THE SECRET GARDEN™

Adapted by Diane Molleson
From the screenplay by Caroline Thompson

SCHOLASTIC INC.
New York Toronto London Auckland Sydney

WARNER BROS. PRESENTS
AN **AMERICAN ZOETROPE** PRODUCTION A FILM BY **AGNIESZKA HOLLAND**
"THE SECRET GARDEN" KATE MABERLY HEYDON PROWSE
ANDREW KNOTT AND **MAGGIE SMITH** MUSIC BY **ZBIGNIEW PREISNER**
EXECUTIVE PRODUCER **FRANCIS FORD COPPOLA** SCREENPLAY BY **CAROLINE THOMPSON**
BASED ON THE BOOK BY **FRANCES HODGSON BURNETT**
PRODUCED BY **FRED FUCHS, FRED ROOS** AND **TOM LUDDY**
DIRECTED BY **AGNIESZKA HOLLAND**

WARNER BROS.
A TIME WARNER ENTERTAINMENT COMPANY
1993 Warner Bros. All Rights Reserved.

ISBN 0-590-47173-2

Designed by Ursula Herzog

12 11 10 9 8 7 6 5 4 3 2   3 4 5 6 7 8/9

Printed in the U.S.A.   37

First Scholastic printing, May 1993

Mary Lennox was ten years old when her life changed forever. Mary lived in India. She was born there and, almost every day, she saw elephants, tigers, snakes, and snake charmers. Her father was an officer in the British army, and her mother, a great beauty, loved to give parties. Both her parents were too busy to pay much attention to Mary. They left her in the care of an Indian nanny, or *ayah,* who dressed her, waited on her, and went with her everywhere.

For all her riches, Mary had no friends. She had an awful temper, and she almost always got her own way. And so, Mary had grown from a spoiled baby into a spoiled, bad-tempered child with mousy brown hair that hung limply around her thin unhappy face.

When a great earthquake struck, many people died, including Mary's parents and *ayah*. Mary was left all alone. So she was sent to live with her uncle, Lord Archibald Craven, at Misselthwaite Manor in England.

Mary traveled from India to England on a big steamship. Other children orphaned in the earthquake traveled with her, but Mary did not like any of them. They didn't like her either.

"She's so sour," a girl named Jenny whispered to her friend Sarah. "I heard she never even cried once about her parents."

When the boat docked in England, Mary looked down at the black swirling water while the other orphans were all met by their relatives or guardians. Finally, a stern-looking woman dressed in black walked up to her. The woman introduced herself as Mrs. Medlock, her uncle's housekeeper.

"My word, she's a plain piece of goods," Mrs. Medlock said to the government official with Mary. "We'd heard her mother was a beauty. She certainly didn't hand much of it down, did she?"

"She might improve as she gets older," the official said kindly. "Children change."

Mary decided right away she did not like Mrs. Medlock.

When they arrived at Misselthwaite Manor, Mary was shown to a large room with an enormous bed. Everything in the manor looked so old and big, Mary felt very small. She did not like her cold room with tapestries on the walls. Nor did she like the moor that stretched around the house for miles and miles and looked like a big black sea.

Mary did not meet her uncle when she arrived. "He's not likely to trouble himself about you," Mrs. Medlock told her. "Since his wife died, he doesn't trouble himself about anyone." Mary was surprised to hear that her aunt, her mother's twin sister, had died.

When Mrs. Medlock brought Mary her breakfast the next morning, she told Mary to stay in her room and not go poking around the manor alone. "There are near one hundred rooms in the house. This one and no other is yours," she said.

"I won't go poking about," Mary answered sullenly.

After Mrs. Medlock left, Mary looked sadly out the window. She could hear the wind howling over the barren moor. But the moaning she heard was not *only* the wind. Mary was sure she could hear someone crying.

Since Mary was not used to obeying anyone, she ignored Mrs. Medlock's orders and opened a little door she had found hidden beneath a tapestry in the far corner of her room. She crawled through it and went down many corridors until she came to a very old part of the manor. Pigeons flew overhead, and the wind rattled broken windows.

Mary saw a door like the little one in her room. Curious, she pushed the door open and walked into a room overgrown with ivy and bare branches. In the corner, she saw a framed photograph on a dressing table. It was a picture of Mary's mother sitting on a garden swing with

her identical twin, Mary's Aunt Lilias.

Mary opened all the drawers in her aunt's dressing table. She found lace handkerchiefs, perfume bottles, and a music box with a large ornate key inside — a key that did not fit any lock in the room.

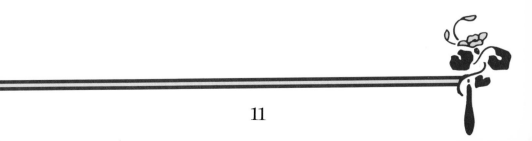

On her way back to her nursery, Mary heard the crying again.

"It's only Lord Craven's dogs," Mrs. Medlock insisted when she caught Mary in the hallway. She grabbed Mary's arm and pulled her up the steep stairs and back to her room. "Now you stay where you're told or I promise you I'll box your ears."

Later that morning, a maid named Martha brought Mary her tea, and helped her dress. "What would you like to wear? Black, black or black?" Martha asked, looking at the row of black dresses in Mary's wardrobe.

"Are you blind? They're all black," Mary said with no sense of humor. Martha couldn't help laughing.

"I won't be laughed at, servant!" Mary screamed harshly.

"My name's Martha," Martha said, feeling sorry for Mary who had no mother or father and was left alone in her room all day. Martha had twelve brothers and sisters and was used to children, though none as rude as Mary.

While Martha served tea, she told Mary all about her younger brother, Dickon, who made friends with many of the animals on the moor, including a wild pony. To Mary's surprise, she found herself liking Martha. She even wondered if she would get to meet Dickon.

That night Mary's uncle came to visit her.
Mary was afraid and pretended to be asleep as
the dark hunched figure of Lord Craven looked
down at her. Lord Craven had a crooked back,
and he looked very sad, as if something had been
troubling him for a long, long time.

The next morning Martha bundled Mary up in
a coat, scarf, and mittens, and sent her outside
to play. The wind was so strong, it almost carried
Mary across the grounds of Misselthwaite Manor.
She walked through many gardens before she
came to a very old wall, overgrown with ivy.

A robin looked down at Mary while she peeked through a crack in the wall. Inside she could see a statue sitting in the middle of a big overgrown garden.

"Where's the door to that one?" Mary asked a gardener, pointing to the ivy covered wall.

"It's shut up," the gardener, whose name was Ben Weatherstaff, answered.

"Where is the door?" Mary demanded.

"No one's been inside for ten years. The dead are dead and gone and better off left that way," Ben answered as he pushed his wheelbarrow away from Mary.

"Who's dead?" Mary asked, following him. "My aunt's dead," Mary continued when Ben would not answer. "It was *her* garden, wasn't it?"

"Don't ask me," Ben said gruffly. "You might as

well ask him." He nodded to a singing robin that had landed beside them. It was the same robin Mary had met at the ivy-covered wall.

The robin moved closer toward Mary and chirped.

Mary wondered why Lord Craven hated her aunt's garden. Why had he kept it locked up ever since she died?

"We're not supposed to talk about it," Martha whispered when Mary asked her.

Mary now went outside almost every day. She looked very hard at the ivy-covered walls for a door, a door that would get her into the closed garden.

One day the robin flew to the old wall and started poking purposefully in some branches of ivy. When Mary pulled back those branches, she uncovered the door. The design near the keyhole looked just like the design on the old key Mary had found in her aunt's dressing room.

Soon Mary was back by the door with the key. She fitted it into the lock and turned it. It took two hands to do it, but the lock finally did turn. Mary took a long breath and looked behind her to see if anyone was coming. Hardly anyone ever did come it seemed, not even the gardeners.

Holding back the swinging curtain of ivy, she pushed the door open, slipped through it, and shut it behind her.

She was standing *inside* the secret garden.

Mary climbed down a long flight of steps to a pond. Everywhere she looked she saw leafless stems of climbing roses. They covered everything — the stone benches, the trees, the walls — in a thick gray mist. There were no roses on the branches now, and Mary did not know if they were dead or alive.

"How still it is," she thought. "I am the first person to come in here for ten years."

The next morning, Mary ate everything on her breakfast plate. "You're sure gettin' on well enough with that this morning," Martha told her.

"It tastes nice today," Mary said between spoonfuls.

Suddenly both Martha and Mary heard a cry above the wailing of the wind.

"Listen. . . . Hear that?" said Mary.

Martha looked nervous. "Poor little Betty Butterworth, the scullery maid. She's had a toothache all morning," she said. Then she hurried Mary out of the house.

Mary could not wait to get back to her garden. As she hurried through the trees, a crow flew up at her. She screamed and ducked.

"Soot," she heard a boy's voice call.

The crow circled and landed on the boy's shoulder.

"He doesn't know you. You frightened him," the boy said.

"I frightened *him*?" Mary answered.

"Come, he won't hurt you. Touch him," the boy insisted.

Mary came slowly toward the boy and crow. The boy was Martha's brother, Dickon.

Dickon knew all about animals. "Sometimes I think I am a bird or a fox or even part beetle," he told Mary. "Animals trust me. They tell me their secrets."

Mary, too, had a secret, and she wanted to tell somebody she could trust.

"I've stolen a garden," she blurted to Dickon. "Maybe it's dead anyhow... I don't know."

"I would know," Dickon said.

"You would?" said Mary.

Dickon nodded.

With his penknife, Dickon cut the dead wood off a rosebush in the secret garden.

"This part's wick. See the green?" he said, touching the cane with the tip of his knife.

"Wick? What's wick?" Mary asked.

"Alive.... Full of life. You'll have so many roses here this summer, you'll be sick of them," he told Mary.

But there was a lot of work to be done. All the old wood needed to be cut away from the roses, and the flower beds needed weeding and seeding.

Mary looked happily around the garden. She would not mind the work. "Look," she said suddenly, spotting an old garden swing. "There's a picture of my mother and my aunt sitting here."

"They say that's how she died," Dickon said.

"How?" Mary asked.

"Falling off it," Dickon answered.

"Oh," said Mary, almost afraid to touch the seat.

That night Mary could not sleep. Again, she heard someone crying.

Taking a candle, she peeked out into the long dark hallway and made sure Mrs. Medlock wasn't coming. Her heart was beating so strongly she felt everyone could hear it, but she followed the sound of the crying until she came to a door covered with a large tapestry.

The crying seemed very near now. She pushed the tapestry door open very gently and found herself face to face with a boy.

"Are you a ghost?" the boy whispered.

"No," Mary whispered back. "Are you?"

"Who are you? What are you doing here?"

"I live here," Mary answered. "Who are you?"

"I am the master of this house while my father is away!"

"Your father? He's my uncle!" Mary cried.

Mary and her cousin, Colin Craven, talked well into the night. They had never known about one another before. Colin was ten years old, just like Mary, but he was sick and stayed in bed all the time. He did not know how to walk and never went outside. He had spent his whole life in his room. He was sure he was going to die.

"Colin's not at all like you," Mary told Dickon as they worked together in the garden. "His cheeks are whiter than ice and marble, whiter than these little hairs," she said, touching the roots of a bulb.

Almost every day, Mary visited Colin when no one was looking. Colin tried to make Mary wear a mask so he would be protected from her germs. Everyone else wore a mask when they saw him,

Medlock's orders. Mrs. Medlock protected Colin from everything.

"I can't stand it," Mary said, tearing off the itchy mask.

"Put it on!" Colin insisted.

"Stop talking to me as if you were a rajah with emeralds and rubies stuck all over you!"

"I'll talk to you any way I please!"

Mary turned away and marched toward the door. "I'm going back outside to be with Dickon."

Colin made a face.

"Dickon knows everything there is to know about gardens," Mary said, wanting also to add *and he's much nicer than you.*

"Does he know about my mother's garden?"

"What?" Mary was caught by surprise. "How would he know about it. It's locked. Nobody's allowed in it."

"Well *I* could make them unlock it."

"No!" Mary shouted. "Don't you see how much better it is if it's a secret?"

Suddenly they both heard Mrs. Medlock's footsteps. Mary dove under the bed and luckily Mrs. Medlock did not catch her. But Martha did and was very upset.

Lord Craven returned from his voyage during the night. The next day, Mary, dressed in her best clothes, was led into the library to meet him. She thought her uncle looked very sad.

"Medlock wants me to send you to some sort of girl's boarding school," Lord Craven muttered.

Mary felt a lump in her throat. "No... please... let me stay," she managed to tell him.

"But there's nothing for a child here."

Mary bit her lip. She did not want to leave.

"I don't need much," Mary said in a small voice. "Could I just have a bit of earth?"

Lord Craven looked puzzled.

"To plant seeds in," Mary said.

To Mary's surprise, Lord Craven laughed. "Take your bit of earth...."

Mary almost skipped out of the library. She would not be sent away. She could stay and watch her garden grow.

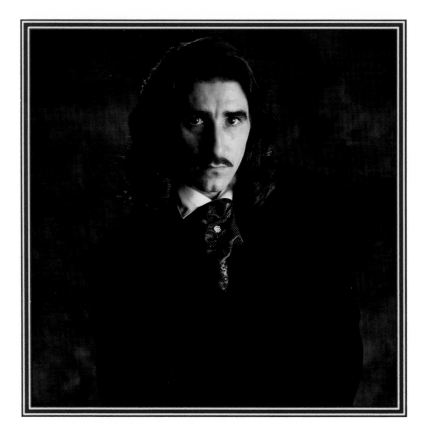

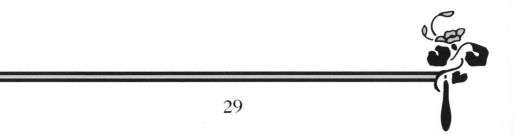

The following day, Lord Craven left on a long trip. He would not be back until fall.

It rained so hard that week, Mary could not work in her garden. Though she often found him rude, she spent many hours with Colin, and he grew used to seeing her.

When the rainstorms ended, Mary did not visit Colin as much. She was too busy working in the garden with Dickon. Colin missed her, and one day he had a terrible tantrum, as terrible as the tantrums Mary used to have in India.

Mary heard his screams outside and rushed to his room. He is so spoiled and rude, she thought. Someone should stand up to him, and it might as well be someone as rude as he was.

"You're so selfish!" Mary screamed at him. You're the most selfish boy there ever was!"

Colin looked so surprised he stopped yelling, but only for a moment. "I'm not as selfish as you are! I'm always ill!"

"Nobody ill could scream like that," Mary retorted.

"I felt a lump on my back. I'll get a lump like my father and. . ."

Before Colin could finish, Mary was by his side, inspecting his back for lumps. She poked and prodded it for a long time.

"There's nothing but your bones sticking out. It's because you're so skinny," she announced.

At that moment, Mrs. Medlock rushed in the room with Martha and John, the footman.

"Get away from him you beastly girl! You'll kill him," she said, lunging at Mary. Mary dodged her and hid behind Colin's pillows.

"She's my cousin," Colin cried, afraid Mrs. Medlock would really hurt Mary. "Now get out of here Medlock. I want to be alone with my cousin."

"I beg your pardon?" Mrs. Medlock looked shocked.

"I'm ordering you to leave this room. Go." Colin said in his most rajahlike tone.

Mrs. Medlock agreed to go, if only to keep Colin calm. But she looked angrier than Mary had ever seen her.

"I'm not ill," Colin said quietly to Mary, as if he still could not quite believe it.

"I don't see how. You're just weak." Mary smiled at him.

"Do you think I could go outside?" Colin asked. "If I went out, we could find the door to my mother's garden."

Mary looked down and bit her lip. She had never told Colin she'd been in the garden. She had never been sure he would keep her secret.

"I've been in the garden," she said softly. "I found the key, weeks ago. . . ."

"Tell me! Go on," he urged.

And so Mary told him all about the robin, the old door, the stone steps, the pond, and the flowers. Colin closed his eyes and fell asleep dreaming of robins and roses.

A few days later, John, the footman, carried Colin downstairs while Mary, Dickon, and many of the servants looked on.

"I am going out in my chair," Colin announced to the staff, many of whom had never seen their young master before. "When I go, no one is to be anywhere about. Not a single gardener," he continued.

"Very good, sir," Roach, the head gardener, replied.

Left to themselves, Dickon pushed Colin's wheelchair across the grounds. Mary and Dickon's animals followed. Colin kept his hands over his eyes until they got all the way down the stone steps in the secret garden.

"Now look," Mary whispered when they neared the pond.

Colin looked and looked as if to make up for ten years of not seeing anything but his room. After the rains, spring had come to the garden, and flowers of every color bloomed around him.

Mary and Dickon stared at Colin. A pink glow had actually spread over his ivory face and neck and hands. "I'm going to come here tomorrow and the day after and the day after that," Colin said, smiling.

"Who is that man?" Colin suddenly asked, pointing to Ben Weatherstaff. Ben was glaring at Mary from the top of a ladder.

"You miserable little heathen," Ben shook his fist at Mary. He could not understand how she had gotten into the garden.

Colin wheeled his chair near Mary. "Do you know who I am?" he asked, sitting up very straight.

"Who you are?" Ben passed his hand across his face. "You're the little cripple," he said.

"I am not a cripple," Colin said firmly.

"Y-your back's not crooked? You haven't got crooked legs?" Ben asked.

"Crooked legs? Who said I had crooked legs?" Colin demanded angrily. His anger made him feel stronger, and he struggled to get out of his chair. Dickon came nearer so Colin could hold his arm. Watching Colin, Mary muttered softly, "You can do it! You can! You can!"

Colin put his thin legs firmly on the ground and slowly pulled himself up until he was standing — straight and tall. He lifted his head back proudly.

It seemed to Mary as though Ben suddenly did something very strange. He choked and put his hands up to his face to wipe the tears streaming down his cheeks.

"Don't say a word about any of this to anyone," Colin said.

Ben sniffed a little and smiled. "I come here before when no one saw me."

"How? Nobody's been inside for ten years," Colin said, still standing.

"I come over the wall. The roses would've died otherwise. Your mother was so fond of this garden. She would ask me in to look after her roses. When she...went away, th' orders were that no one was to come here, but I come anyway. She gave her orders first."

"I'm glad you did." Colin told him. "You'll know how to keep a secret."

"Eh, lad," Ben answered.

From that day on, Colin went out to the garden almost every day. He practiced standing, and bit by bit he learned to walk.

One day Colin visited Mary in her room. Mary was very surprised he had been able to climb the stairs all by himself.

"This is just how I want it to be with my father. I'll walk into his room and I'll say 'It's me Father... I'm here,'" said Colin.

"But he's not due back for a long time," Mary reminded him.

"I'm ready now. I want him to see me before anyone else does."

Not long afterward, Lord Craven had a dream. In his dream, he saw his wife and heard her voice calling him to the garden. He woke with a start and rushed home to the manor.

Purple heather, yellow gorse, and fresh spots of green grass bloomed on the moor, but Lord Craven barely noticed. When his carriage pulled up at the house, he hurried inside to see his son. He felt sure something had happened to Colin, and he feared the worst.

"Where's my son?" Lord Craven almost growled to Mrs. Medlock when he couldn't find Colin in his room.

"He should be here," Mrs. Medlock said, staring at Colin's empty bed. Immediately she blamed Mary. "It's that child, my lord. She must be sent away. She'll kill Colin for sure."

"Take me to her room."

"Mary, your uncle's here," Mrs. Medlock called. But Mary's room was empty as well.

"I beg your pardon my lord. Perhaps they're in the garden," Martha said, coming up the stairs.

"In the garden..." Lord Craven repeated. Suddenly he knew exactly where they were. "You stay here," he warned Mrs. Medlock.

Lord Craven heard laughter as he approached the secret garden.

Inside the garden, Colin was blindfolded. Mary and Dickon spun him around and around. "Now come get us," Mary called, giggling. Colin took a few blind steps forward.

Lord Craven opened the door. Not until he had gone down the long flight of steps did he see his son. He stared openmouthed as Colin walked around the garden blindfolded.

Mary peeked out of her hiding place. When she saw Lord Craven, she put her hand over her mouth and gestured to Dickon to look too.

Colin circled the garden and came toward Lord Craven, feeling his way with his hands. Colin touched his father's chest, then reached up and felt his face. With trembling hands, he pulled down his blindfold and stared up at his father.

"I can't believe it," Lord Craven finally said. He hugged his son for a long, long time.

To Mary, it seemed as if Lord Craven looked right at her, then away again. Colin now had his father. What would happen to her? She slipped out the door, barely able to keep from crying.

Mary was all the way out on the moor when she heard her name being called above the wind. "Mary, Ma-a-ry... Mary, why are you out here by yourself," Lord Craven asked, coming toward her.

Mary shrugged and tried to stop crying. "It was shut up," she said through her tears.

"What was shut up?" asked Lord Craven.

"The garden," Mary answered.

"But thanks to you, Mary," he said, "it will never be shut up again. You've brought us all back to life." He hugged the little girl.

Smiling, she hugged him back. Colin ran out to join them, and the three of them hugged. The secret garden had worked its magic. Smiling and laughing and holding hands, they went back inside together.